W9-BHR-838

Around the Year

A picture book
by Elsa Beskow

Floris Books

First published in Swedish in 1927 as *Årets Saga*
First published in English in 1988 by Floris Books
15 Harrison Gardens, Edinburgh
Eighth printing 2010

British Library CIP data available
ISBN 978-086315-075-3
Printed in Belgium

THE MONTHS

January begins the year,
February is next.
March and April, wind and rain,
May and June with sun again,
July and August summer months.
Autumn brings September
and October, too.
Then grey November,
and December ends the year.

THE HOURS

One and Two
are walking.
Three and Four
are playing.
Five and Six
are eating.
Seven and Eight
run out to play.
Nine and Ten
are cutting hay.
Eleven and Twelve
are — whoopsie-daisy —
upside down!

THE DAYS OF THE WEEK

Tell me what do you do all day?
Busy, I am, but listen pray!
MONDAY is my milking day
TUESDAY skimming off the cream
WEDNESDAY's when the butter's churned
And packed away each THURSDAY
FRIDAY's when I bake all day
SATURDAY is market day
On SUNDAY off to church I plod
Thanks be to Thee, Almighty God.

JANUARY

Tick-tock says the clock,
it's twelve of the night.
The New Year's here
and the stars are bright.

The old year's gone,
he's tired and worn.
Christmas is past,
the tree all shorn.

The star-children come
in the dead of night,
like Three Wise Men
bringing the light.

Tick-tock says the clock.
The New Year's come.
Good Year to you all
until the next to come.

EB

FEBRUARY

Blue skies and ice
wherever we go,
slipping and sliding
deep in the snow.

Uphill and downhill,
neither leaf nor green:
the sun bright and clear,
no grass to be seen.

Woollies and hoods,
on toboggans all day.
Gloves on our hands
and Spring far away.

Back home Mama's baking
big loaves and small.
How hungry we are —
we'll soon eat them all!

EB

March is an old man,
old and cold,
grey beard and weary.
He sits there
melting the snow,
tempting the catkins,
the pussy-willow twigs,
watched by the coltsfoot,
the first signs of Spring.

Soon he'll be going,
the grass will turn green.
Soon warm sun
will melt him,
and he will be gone.

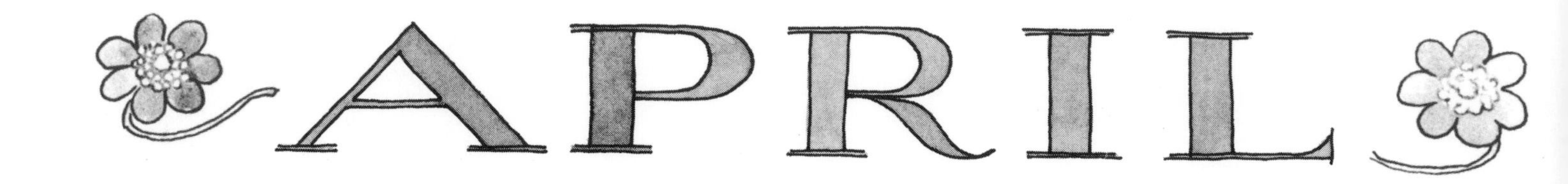

April, April,
the snow is gone.
April, April,
the flowers have come.

April, April,
green and brown,
bells on your collar
and willow on crown.

April, April,
watch the sky,
the showers are sweet,
but soon go by.

April, April,
where are your leaves?
Soon,
soon
they'll be here,
for winter's gone
and Spring is near.

May comes but once a year,
the dancing month,
the sky light and high,
the birch trees bursting.
May-daisy time,
and cowslip
and primrose
and harebell
and dancing anemones.
Deep down in the meadow grass,
they're all dancing
with delight,
lily-of-the-valley
nodding,
ringing her bells,
the silver trunks
lordly and slim,
their branches and silvery twigs
dancing
too
to the tune of Spring.

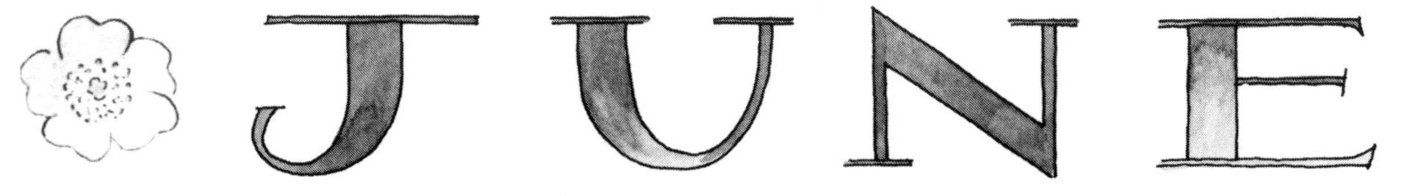

First Summer is here,
the lake so mild.
Summer has come
to the water-child.

We'll take the boat
and row to an isle.
We'll bathe in the water,
leave our clothes in a pile.

We'll play at boats,
we'll splash and tease.
The sun is so warm
and so is the breeze.

A June day it is
when all is green.
We'll row through the reeds
and never be seen.

First summer is here,
the lake is so mild.
Summer has come
to the water-child.

EB

The sun is hot,
for July is here,
haymaking time
in the fields.
Now is the time
when
cabbages grow,
the spinach
and cress,
the lettuce and onions
and leeks.

Now is the time
when each day
I go to the pump
with my
watering-can
and water and water
the rows.
The poppies glow red,
tiger-lilies gold,
the grasses
are tall and straight.

But July is here
and
THUNDER in the air.

AUGUST

August — the time of ripeness,
the corn glowing,
the berries all ripening.

The magpie stands guard,
watching
the bilberries,
the raspberries,
blackberries,
cranberries
and gooseberries,
the red and black currants,
the whortleberries,
cloudberries and more.

They dance in a ring,
the Berry Queen smiling,
clad in her August array.

And the magpie —
he just watches.

For he's not interested
in August.

He's hungry.

SEPTEMBER

Dear apple, on your branch,
please fall into my hat.
For if I take you off the tree,
They'll not be pleased with that!

Apples red and apples green,
please fall down upon the ground.
For if I pick you off the tree,
I cannot say how you've been found.

Apples here and apples there,
please fall into my hand.
My little sisters stand and stare
and wait for you to land.

Hips and haws and thistles tall
stand all around the tree.
All will soon be picked and stored.
Is there not just one for me?

Apples, apples, everywhere,
please let me have just one,
and just two more, please, tree,
then September will be done.

Golden, you are,
October.
Golden sovereigns on your trees.
Golden guineas on your floor,
golden coins of leaves
that fall
for us to scuffle through
and rustle
and rattle
and hustle
and scrabble
and dabble
and paddle
as they fall
into an October carpet
which hides
our shoes.

Grey is November,
cold as cold.
Stormy November,
wind and rain.
No snow.
No ice.
No glittering sun.
Grey is November,
except
by the bright fire
with a story,
a cushion for the cat,
the dark shut outside
and
the light in the flames
where mysteries lie
and
we dream.

NOVEMBER
10

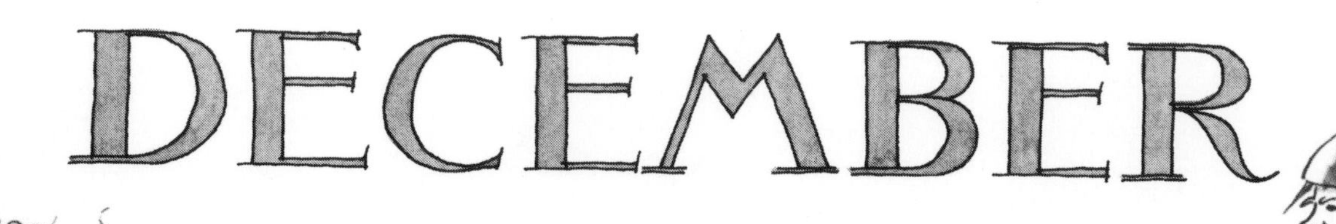

DECEMBER

Christmas is here again,
the tree on its way,
Lucia in her candled crown,
the family all dancing.
Santa comes with laden sack.
The snow falls thick and fast.
Christmas is here again
with parcels
and presents
and candles
and cake
and magic
and lights in the windows.
It is Christmas
— a feast,
a festival,
of Christ.